Pastor Ed Smith

Blessings

Solomon

THE FALLEN STONE

Purpose is often found
at rock bottom

Terri McFaddin-Solomon

WESTBOW·
P R E S S
A DIVISION OF THOMAS NELSON
& ZONDERVAN

WestBow Press books may be ordered through
booksellers or by contacting:

WestBow Press
A Division of Thomas Nelson & Zondervan
1663 Liberty Drive
Bloomington, IN 47403
www.westbowpress.com
1 (866) 928-1240

ISBN: 978-1-4908-6305-4 (sc)
ISBN: 978-1-4908-6304-7 (e)

Library of Congress Control Number: 2014921971

Print information available on the last page.

WestBow Press rev. date: 2/18/2015

CONTENTS

ENDORSEMENTS

This is a God-inspired read filled with deep, rich insights. It is fast paced, entertaining and thoughtful. As a creative writing partner, I know firsthand that Terri is a never-ending reservoir of God ideas.

—Philip Bailey,
Lead singer, Earth, Wind and Fire

The Fallen Stone is an earthly story with a heavenly, eternal meaning. Read this allegorical tale of "Peak," the fallen stone. Its wit will capture your imagination and release you to see and understand the truth—God can even take your most difficult circumstances, even your failures, and use them to mold and shape you to achieve your destiny. This book is a must read.

—Bishop Gideon A. Thompson
New Covenant Church, Boston, MA.

On the surface, *The Fallen Stone* is a light and witty tale that grows deeper with each page and chapter. Although the main focus is about a stone falling from the top and landing on the bottom, the deeper story is about the relationships that are formed along the way. Please don't miss the surprise ending— you won't be disappointed.

—Deborah Smith Pegues,
Bestselling author of thirty books

DEDICATION

Thank you, Lord Jesus for *The Fallen Stone*
For my blessed-and-highly-favored
husband, Charles Solomon
My helping-hands, Janet Bailey and
Michelle McKinney Hammond,
Paul, Michaela, Rick, Roslyn, Darryl,
Theresa, Grace, Adam, Kate, Chloe,
Ashley Jade, Anthony, Todd and Manny

FOREWORD

Terri has a way of weaving a story that pulls you into the experience causing you to personalize the events. The depth of revelation hits you in the deepest part of your core. *The Fallen Stone* innocently pokes fun at our ego and our desire to be counted in the world. It deals with our failed expectations and disappointments and then gloriously gives us hope that God can redeem our brokenness and use us in a way that creates a winning legacy beyond what we could ever dream.

This book is destined to become a timeless classic that you will read from time to time and will be shared with generations to come. *The Stone* is a gift from God to you as well as those you love.

Michelle McKinney Hammond,
Best selling author –
Getting Smart About Life, Love and Men

The Fallen Stone is a book that everyone will enjoy reading – no matter what age or gender.

A NOTE FROM TERRI

The Fallen Stone is the story of my personal journey written in the form of an allegory. It is also the story of countless people that have hit rock bottom, only to rise again.

When I found myself sprawled out on the ground of failure, I was embarrassed and ashamed. I thought I would never recover. Little did I know that GOD'S CALL OFTEN STARTS WITH A FALL.

Romans 8:28 reminds us that all things are working together for good to those who love God, to those who are the called according to His purpose.

Many of you already know that God loves surprise parties. He can turn on the lights in the darkest hour of your life and yell, "surprise!" That's when you discover that your tragedy has turned into a triumph and your mess-up becomes a miracle. Surprise! Surprise!

If you should experience a fall in life, here's the good news paraphrased in Psalm 37:24 – Though you fall, you will not be utterly cast down, the Lord will pick you back up with his hand.

The Fallen Stone is the story of falling down and getting back up again. It is a time of building faith, gaining wisdom and increasing in spiritual maturity.

So be encouraged. Your latter days will be greater than your former.

SHALOM
Terri McFaddin-Solomon

You're invited to visit:
Terri's Blog Page – HOPE STREET
www.Hopestreetblog.org
#Thefallensstone
Email: Tmcfaddinsolomon@gmail.com
Office: 310.327.4151

CHAPTER 1

THE FALL

The dawn of a new day filled the morning sky, and a towering mountain known throughout the region as "Peak" smiled as he surveyed the vast terrain that lay at his majestic feet. It was that time of year when the earth was slowly turning to a gentler season, forcing winter to relinquish its icy grip.

To celebrate this event, springtime dressed herself in yellow and purple wildflowers and danced across the hillsides to the music of singing birds and lovesick foxes.

What a glorious day, Peak thought as

he took a deep breath, inhaling the sweet fragrance of the crisp morning air.

Peak was happy and secure in his position. It was very peaceful looking out over the vast valley, especially from such a place of prominence. Yes, he felt very powerful indeed. After all, the sun could not be seen in the morning until it rose over his expansive summit. In the winter months, the snow did not fall in the valley, because Peak would catch it on his strong shoulders and hold it in his stony bosom until the early spring. Then, at the appointed time, the melting snow would be gently released into the thirsty riverbeds below.

From time to time, eagles would attempt to fly upward to build a nest at the top of Peak's lofty domain. Peak watched with amusement as one of the fearless birds struggled against the air currents that surrounded the top of the mountain like an invisible fortress. The violent winds gripped the great bird and howled with laughter as the challenger struggled to break free. In the end, the eagle spiraled downward to a place where the breeze blew gently against his battered wings.

There were other challengers who put themselves to the test. The mountain goats with their strong bodies and sure footing also tried to reach Peak's place of prominence and dominance. A few fearless goats had made their way to the higher grounds filled with dangerous pockets of bottomless snow and sheets of treacherous ice. But it always ended with a slip of the foot that sent the poor mountain goats plunging to a terrible end. There were many more attempts, but no one ever reached the very top of the mountain and lived to tell about it.

Only the clouds above had the privilege of sharing the sky with the arrogant Peak. No matter how hard they tried, Peak made no alliance with the clouds and avoided their company as much as possible. This was because he knew their true nature. Behind their peaceful, smiling, and billowy faces, they could be treacherous and unpredictable.

Sometimes, the clouds were filled with refreshing dew and rain. This was most appreciated during the long, hot, summer days. At other times, without warning, the clouds turned dark and angry, bringing furious rainstorms or blinding ice and snow.

As if driven by a mysterious fit of rage, the ominous clouds sometimes spewed hailstones that exploded like missiles against the face of Peak. Without mercy, the icy stones beat against the mountain and then crashed and melted in the earth below.

"We meant no harm," the clouds would always apologize after the calm had been restored. "But when the freezing winds push and swirl us in every direction, we get all worked up and things get a little out of control."

In spite of the cloud's feigned apologies, Peak knew too well that they lived and breathed to intimidate and dominate everything under the heavens.

Even with the attacks of wind, rain, snow, and hail, Peak remained proud, strong, and silent, never showing any signs of weakness. He reigned over mountains, hills, and valleys below, declaring to both friends and foes, "I shall never be moved!"

But as time passed, there came a difficult winter with its army of violent storms. The earth hid its face as the storms attack without mercy.

"So this proud, arrogant mountaintop thinks he can't be moved!" the storm clouds grumbled to one another as they beat against Peak with blizzards of hail, ice, rain, and snow.

Peak scoffed. "Send your thunder and lightning! Send your hail and snow! I shall never be moved! I… and I alone rule the sky! And this too shall pass!"

Little did Peak know that the deposits of icy rain had seeped deep into the cracks and crevices of his strong shoulders. When the water froze, it expanded, forcing the cracks to separate even more. He could feel the pain as the crevices grew deeper and deeper. Even though there was pain, Peak stood tall and strong in the face of the attacks and continued to declare, "I shall never be moved!"

Still, the cracks grew deeper, the winds blew stronger, and the weight of the ice and snow grew heavier and heavier. On the outside, Peak remained strong and stoic, but deep inside, he knew that he was carrying much more than he was able to bear.

One night, in the cold, still dead of winter, something that felt like devouring fangs gripped him. It was a force that seemed to rise from the depths of hell, looming larger than the mountain or the sky. Without mercy, it ripped into the heart of the mountain. Peak reeled and cried out in anguish.

He desperately prayed for someone to wake him from this terrible nightmare. "Dear Lord, don't allow my enemies to triumph over me," he silently prayed.

It seemed like an eternity as the pain and pressure continued their journey deep into the cracks and crevices of the terrified Peak.

The God who created the mountains, the sky, the clouds, and the storm did not speak. Nor did He hold back the ice, rain, and snow, or come to Peak's rescue.

As the night wore on and the relentless blizzard continued, suddenly there was a stillness in the air. In that moment, what Peak thought could never ever happen happened. It seemed as if the whole earth was moving in slow motion as the top of Peak's body broke into a giant splinter of rock and began to tumble downward.

To the delight of the dark clouds and the shock of all creatures below, Peak tumbled down, down, down, and down again, hurling past the lower peaks that he had once looked down on with quiet arrogance. Past the nesting eagles that had never had the privilege of looking into the face of the great mountain peak. Past the sure-footed goats that ran for cover as the massive rock, with all of its debris, continued its swift descent from the top.

Finally, what was left of Peak came to rest in the valley below, never to rise again.

CHAPTER 2

ROCK BOTTOM

For a long time, Peak lay silent and desolate. It seemed like an eternity passed as the seasons came and went in the valley. The snow and the rain fell both hard and soft. The scorching sun beat down on what was left of Peak's face. Lizards and snakes nestled beneath his shoulders, and still Peak was silent.

One day, the kindhearted valley spoke out, talking as if he was engaging in just one of the many conversations with the fallen mountaintop. "Did you know there is life after a fall?"

Peak was somewhat startled but did not answer. He might have been angry at the intrusion, but anger was a feeling, and the desire to feel anything had passed away in the winters of long ago. But at the end of the day, just as the sun was setting, Peak decided to respond. "What is your name? And what would you know about a fall?"

"Well, well, welcome to my humble domain. My name is Valor, and most of the treasures from above fall right into my lap. That's how I know about falls. Once, long ago, I even caught a falling star. With all of its brightness in the heavens above, I thought sure that star would light up the entire valley, but when it landed, it was nothing more than a large piece of smoldering rock. What a disappointment."

Peak was not impressed with Valor's story. "I take it that you've never experienced a personal fall."

Valor smiled to himself. "I wasn't always

a valley. Once I was a mountain peak just like you, and even higher, I might add. I was given the name Valor because I was mighty and fearless. I triumphed over the elements of the sky and all of their hateful attacks. But over the centuries, the storms of life took their toll and I learned a lesson that can only be learned from a fall."

"And what lesson is that?" asked Peak.

"Wherever we climb to, or wherever we fall from, we are still in God's hands."

A heaviness began to sweep over Peak. "What good does it do to be in God's hands in this broken condition?"

Now the feelings were coming back like a sleeping foot or hand waking with a sensation of stinging needles. There was pain and discomfort and Peak could feel it gaining momentum.

"To be broken is just the beginning of your journey," Valor answered. "It took more than you could imagine for a strong-willed mountain peak like me to be refined into fertile topsoil. I fought it with everything in me. Little did I know that the more I fought against God's will, the more He used my resistance to shape me into what He intended all along.

"At first, I was ashamed of what I had become. It was difficult to see the benefit of my transformation. But once I let go of the past and embraced the future, I soon became a very contented, productive valley.

"Everything grows here," Valor said proudly. "I am the storage place for falling rain, and together, we nourish the seeds that are planted here. Because I am the source that brings about the desire of others, my life is full and rewarding."

Peak was still not impressed. In spite of the beautiful words, in his eyes, Valor was still nothing more than a pile of dirt.

Valor could almost read Peak's mind. "Fertile soil is where I find joy and fulfillment. Your destiny could lie in countless other possibilities. Wherever life takes you, I know that everything works together to fulfill the purpose of God."

Peak could feel his anger rising. "Must we talk about God, the great almighty one who amuses Himself by playing games with all creation? I can just picture Him sitting on His royal throne saying, 'Let's dry up an ocean today! That will teach those big, bossy, whales a lesson or two.' 'No! I think I have a better idea,' says the Almighty. 'Let's topple a mountain peak, crush him, and break him. Then we'll watch as he tries to figure out how to climb back up to the top. Ha, ha!'

"I understand your pain." Valor tried to comfort Peak. "It may not look like it right now, but I know that God has a plan to bring good out of your downfall and not evil."

"What kind of plan could be as great as being a great mountain peak? Just name one thing."

Valor thought for a moment and then answered, "Well, you are still a magnificent-looking rock."

"A rock! Did you call me a rock?" Peak was furious as the truth penetrated like a sharp knife.

"I meant no offense, but I have seen great rocks taken away to build pyramids and palaces for kings. Others are used to build monuments and memorials to remind people of their history. Sometimes, great rocks are used to build a place to worship God," Valor explained.

Peak's anger continued. "None of what you mentioned compares with being a mountain peak! I looked down on the palaces of kings. And as for the memorial stones, in just a few generations, no one will remember why it was even there in the first place. As for a place of worship, when one looks at a mighty mountain peak standing taller than any human could ever dream of reaching, how could you not worship God?"

"Excuse me!" a voice interrupted. It was a massive gray bolder glaring down at Peak. "Do I detect that this waking giant thinks he's too good to be called an ordinary rock?"

At first, Peak was silent as the stranger continued his rebuke. "I've met your type before. You're were so high and mighty that you forgot about all the rocks and stones and dirt that supported you and held you up so you could stand taller than all of us. Now you must face the painful truth. You are nothing more than a broken piece of granite, just like me."

Peak was indignant. "So you're blaming me because I had the guts to rise above you and the others? You're angry because I chose to become the biggest and best?"

The granite rock laughed. "You are so arrogant that you've deceived yourself into believing that your rise to the top was all your own doing. No matter how great you think you are, success only comes with the support of others."

"You really expect me to be grateful to a worthless pile of dirt?" Peak said.

The granite was fuming but kept his composure. "Everything in creation has a purpose. Dirt and rocks are the foundation of roads that join cities and nations together. But for all of our efforts, we are still treated as if we have no value at all. If the truth were told, it is the dirt and rocks that hold the whole world together."

"Well, three cheers for the dirt and the rocks!" Peak mocked.

The granite rock became angrier and

angrier. "It never changes. The dirt and the rocks do all the work while mountain peaks sit in their ivory towers taking all the credit and reaping all the glory. Well, you're not at the top anymore, smugly looking down on everyone else. Welcome to the real world, Mr. Has-Been!"

Peak was at the boiling point. He had never known such blatant disrespect. "Why you worthless piece of stone," he fumed. "Even as a broken peak, I'm ten times more powerful than you could ever hope to be!"

The granite was furious. He shook and reeled back and forth until he was airborne, soaring through the air and falling down on top of Peak with the impact of a meteorite. The entire valley shook as the massive granite rock fell on top of Peak, splitting him into large pieces of stone.

At first, Peak struggled beneath the weight of the heavy granite. Then he became still and smiled to himself. The angry granite had done him a favor. He helped him to escape from the cares of the world and buried him in a quiet unmarked grave.

CHAPTER 3

FACING REJECTION

Years later, as another winter was coming to a close and small patches of the melting snow covered the rocks, a large wagon passed through the valley. A group of men with hammers in their hands climbed down from the wagon and walked over to the pile of rocks and stones. They carefully studied the rocks, rubbing their hands across their surfaces and then tapping them with their hammers. Some of the soft porous stones crumbled as soon as the hammer struck them.

Peak, who had been quietly buried beneath the other rocks, was startled by the strange sounds. At first, he thought it might be small rocks sliding down the mountain. But if this was true, then why did he feel so nervous and uneasy?

Suddenly, there was a thin stream of light and hands reaching in, pushing aside the dirt and dead leaves, allowing more light and cold air to pour into Peak's unmarked grave.

"Looks like a good piece of stone," a man spoke out. Without warning, Peak was hit with a sharp blow. He cringed as the hammer continued to strike.

"Perfect! This one is perfect!" The blows suddenly stopped. A large, violating hand rubbed the surface of Peak. Long ago, he stood so far above the earth that he never dreamed of being touched by human hands. But now he was being handled against his will, and the humiliation was more than he could bear.

"Is it large enough?" one of the men asked.

"Yes, it is perfect for the job," a second man answered.

The two men dug around Peak and then tied him with ropes. With an enormous amount of effort, they pulled Peak out of the dirt and loaded him onto the back of a wagon. Peak was so paralyzed with fear that his mind slipped into a great gulf of darkness.

An entire day had passed when Peak finally opened his eyes again. The sky was filled with dark clouds of dust that blocked the sun. The wagon stopped for a moment as a large, rusted, iron gate opened in front of the wagon. Soon, they were moving again slowly through the gate, where the pounding sound grew louder and louder. The noise vibrated through the wheels of the wagon, making Peak's heart tremble with fear. The two men removed Peak from the wagon and sat him against a wall. Across from where Peak was resting stood a stack of small, perfectly cut stones lined up in order. The group of stones stared in unison at Peak.

"Where am I?" Peak was choking from

the heavy dust as he addressed the group of stones.

"I think we are the ones who should be asking the questions," the leader of the cut stones said as he frowned at Peak. "Who are you? And where did you come from?"

Peak looked down at himself, then back at the leader of the stones. "I don't know who I am anymore. I was once a mountain peak, but those days are far behind me now."

"Imagine that!" the leader taunted. "A real live mountain peak right here in our humble quarry.

"And what mountain were you *peeking* over?" one of the stones joked.

Peak swallowed his pride. "So what exactly is a quarry?" he asked.

"Poor fellow. Are you joking?" one of the stone's countered.

Peak breathed deeply, trying to hide his frustration. "No, I'm not. Please, explain to me about this place you call a quarry."

"I see. You really don't know," the leader of the stones replied. "A quarry is a place where stones are dug out of the earth and turned into building materials. Some stones are made into walls, while others are used to build buildings and even bridges."

Peak listened with great interest. "But what about the stones that don't become walls or houses? What happens to them?" he asked.

There was a moment of silence, and then the leader whispered. "Do you hear the hammering? Do you see the billows of the dust?"

Peak nodded.

As with one voice, the stack of cut stones whispered together, "It's the gravel pit."

"The gravel pit?" Peak was dumbfounded.

Once again, the leader spoke. "The great hammer will test us all. If you are weak and unable to withstand the blows, then you will be broken and crushed until there is nothing left of you except small chips of dirt and gravel. For the rest of your life, you will lay upon the roads that lead from one place to another. You will be stepped on, spit on, abused, and degraded by men and beasts. The rain will fall so hard that you will be forced to swallow mud and dirt. The blistering heat will torment you and turn you into burning cinders. Without a doubt, it's a fate worse than death."

Peak swallowed hard as he listened to the sound of the hammer and stared at the stones in disbelief.

Suddenly, the leader's demeanor completely changed. "We still can't imagine why anyone would drag you into a limestone quarry when you are clearly a granite stone."

As the leader of the stones continued, Peak grew more and more confused.

"It's true that granite is harder than lime, but we certainly are in no way inferior. Limestone was used to build most of the great pyramids of Egypt. Our reputation precedes us around the world."

Peak was learning more in these few moments than he had in centuries as a mountain peak. Just as he was about to ask another question that might help him understand why he had been brought to this terrible place, he was interrupted.

Two men were talking in loud voices and walking in his direction. One of the men was waving his hands and banging things as he talked. "I don't need this stone! As far as I'm concerned, you can dump it into the gravel pit!"

The second man waved his finger in the opposing man's face. "If we are going to build a strong structure, then you know as well as I do that we must have a sturdy cornerstone. The granite is harder than the limestone! That's why I insist on using this particular stone." He pointed at Peak.

The first man was furious. "We don't need a granite cornerstone!"

Now the two men were face-to-face and eye-to-eye.

"I'm the architect, and I say granite!"

"And I'm the master builder, and I say no!"

"Granite! It's stronger!" the architect raised his fist in protest.

"We'll see about that." The master builder stormed away.

Later that night when the quarry was frightfully still, four men appeared carrying ropes. They were completely silent as they lifted Peak and maneuvered him onto a wide slab. Peak was filled with dread as the men carefully studied his surface and then marked him with a series of dark charcoal lines. What came next could only be compared to the terrible night when Peak came crashing down from the top of the mountain.

Using long, iron spikes, the men lifted their hammers high then brought them down with piercing blows. After making a series of holes, they used razor-sharp chisels and began to size and cut Peak into a perfectly measured cornerstone.

Physical pain was one thing, but Peak was feeling something much deeper. It was the pain of betrayal and desertion. Once again, God had forsaken him and allowed him to fall into enemy hands.

"Never again will I trust you or put my faith in you." Peak made a silent declaration to God. "Never again!"

When the process was completed, the four men washed Peak down in cool water, loaded him onto a wagon, and carried away to an unknown destination.

Peak was numb to the uproar that erupted when the wagon arrived at the building site.

The limestone bricks were everywhere, shaking their fists and protesting loudly as Peak was carried to the center of the building site.

"Away with him!" the limestone chanted in unity.

Carefully, the men placed the newly cut cornerstone at the feet of the master builder. A great hush fell over the crowd.

"Well, my friend, you have made your journey in vain." The builder glared at the freshly cut stone. "The architect that insisted on using you is not here. You are in my hands now. And you will never be the cornerstone in this building."

The limestone went into a joyful frenzy as the master builder spit at Peak then ordered the men to remove him from the building site.

The four men grumbled at the unwanted task. With careless hands, they loaded Peak back onto the wagon and departed.

"How can we get rid of this rock?" one of the men asked the others. The driver thought for a moment. "Well, if the best place to hide a tree is in the forest, then the best place to hide a rock is in the mountains."

The sun was fading as the squeaking wagon wheels carrying Peak climbed the steep hill, following the road that led higher and higher up the mountainside.

"Look! There is a cave just ahead," one of the men announced. "A good place to dump this worthless piece of rock."

The four men moved the wagon close to the mouth of the cave then roughly dumped Peak just inside the opening.

One of the men stopped and looked at Peak with a hint of pity in his eyes. "I know it hurts to be thrown away, but man's rejection is God's protection."

The man returned to the wagon with the others and drove away. All through the night, Peak lay in the darkness of the cave, grateful that no one could hear his mournful sobs.

CHAPTER 4

THE GREAT PRETENDER

A few months after the men left Peak in the abandoned cave, he woke to the sound of chanting voices. He was more curious than afraid. Through the pale streaks of daylight, he could make out the images of strange-looking men in black robes. Peak watched with great curiosity as the men whispered to one another while making signs with their hands.

"At last, he has come!" one of them cried out with joy.

For a long time, they carefully examined Peak, running their boney fingers over the carved markings that were made by the men in the quarry. They whispered to each other in a strange language then went away. The next day, the same men appeared at the mouth of the cave with a large wagon decorated with flowers and green vines.

The men carefully lifted Peak onto the wagon, singing and chanting as they struggled up the mountain road. Finally, the wagon passed through a beautiful, golden gate. Music played on string instruments, and the strong smell of incense filled the air. A group of men dressed in long, colorful robes, with symbols tattooed onto their foreheads and hands, approached the wagon. Moments later the men untied Peak and carried him into a courtyard with floors inlaid with precious stones and tall marble pillars that seemed to reach to heaven. A mysterious calm came over Peak as the excited men whispered among themselves. He had already endured the ultimate suffering; now he simply wondered what would be his next cross to bear.

In the days that followed, men and women in elaborate robes surrounded Peak. They sang strange songs, smiling and bowing to Peak as they came in and out of the courtyard. They laid flowers at his feet and sprinkled him with a thick, red liquid that smelled like the blood of animals.

Soon a group of women with long, black hair brought a bag of tools and stood in front of Peak. Slowly and gently, they began to carve and chisel pictures on Peak's surface.

There was hardly any pain. Just their annoying pounding and probing mingled with the strange songs the workers continued to sing.

When they finished chiseling and cutting, the strongest of the men carefully moved Peak to a high platform beneath the open sky. Peak sat on the edge of a cliff overlooking a crystal-blue river that ran through the lush valley below. His heart leaped with joy as he took in the panoramic view. With the exception of the mountains that loomed overhead, it was almost as if Peak had been completely restored to his original place of prominence.

Throngs of people gathering in the courtyard quickly interrupted his blissful moment.

"Our god has come! At last, our god has come!" the people shouted as they danced around Peak. "His image is perfect. He came to earth and dwelled in a cave just as the writings said he would. He knew that we would find him there. Praise be to our god!"

The man with the long, white beard stood on a platform next to Peak and began to lead the people in a chant.

They think I'm a god! Peak thought.

The women laid flowers and fruit at his feet and gently kissed the beautifully carved idol. Men brought gold, silver, and precious stones, then fell on their faces and prayed to Peak.

"We love you!" they softly cried out. "We love you, oh great lord of the mountain."

Peak's mind reeled. Deep inside, he still knew the truth: a carved piece of stone was no match for the one and only, true living God.

In spite of the pain he suffered and his angry feelings toward God, Peak was appalled that people would fall at his feet and give all their earthly possessions just to be in his presence.

But as time passed, another voice inside of him grew stronger. "You've suffered enough. You deserve to be loved, admired, and yes, even worshiped. After all, isn't this your true calling?"

As the admiration toward Peak continued, the voice inside of him grew stronger and bolder. "It is only natural that people would worship you. You have always been a god! When you dwelled at the top of the mountain, you were a god. Here on the hillside, you are still a god. Only now, the people can touch you, love you, and show their appreciation for all you have done for them."

By the time summer was in full bloom, the crops grew in abundance like never before. People, of course, attributed their good fortune to the presence of Peak, their beloved god. The more the villages prospered, the more Peak's fame grew and the more devotees came from far and near to worship him. There was an abundance of gold and silver that could barely be counted. Everything and anything that could be imagined or desired was brought to the great Peak and laid at his feet.

Of course, Peak no longer resisted the voice inside of him that made him believe he was a god. The rich and poor, the young and old, continued to bring sweet sacrifices. They stood before him singing, praying, and speaking words of love. Finally, with the continuous adoration and praise from the people, Peak convinced himself that he was indeed a god.

Early one morning while Peak sat quietly basking in his own glory, a blackbird fluttered into the courtyard and began to eat the succulent red grapes that were sitting on the altar. Peak was quite annoyed, so he rumbled a little, hoping the pesky bird would fly away.

The blackbird was startled for a moment. He looked up at Peak seemingly amused. "I only fear the living," the blackbird said as he continued to eat from the basket. Peak fumed as the bird finished eating then fluttered around his face and landed on his head.

"Have you ever ask yourself why people worship you? After all, you cannot speak to them, so you cannot give them advice or wise counsel. You certainly cannot help them if trouble should arise. So what good are you?" The blackbird hovered directly in front of Peak's face, taking a closer look at his elaborate carvings.

Peak grew even more furious. In spite of his displeasure, he spoke in a calm, dignified tone, reflective of his exalted position. "People worship me because I bless them and watch over them. I bring them good fortune."

The blackbird laughed out loud. "Unbelievable! There is no one more deceived than he who deceives himself. And you are completely deceived."

Peak was losing patience. "How dare you! You blasphemous creature, leave my presence now! Or you will regret it."

"And what are going to do if I don't leave?" the blackbird mocked. "You have no power.

Can't you see that these people only pretend to worship you?"

"Pretend?" Peak railed. "Look at my altar. It is filled with gifts of gratitude to me, their god."

The blackbird landed on the altar and clumsily knocked over a golden cup of sacred wine. He looked up at Peak. "If you were a real god, you would have laws and a certain standards of behavior like the Ten Commandments. But these people make up their own laws because you are only a piece of stone. You don't have the power to interfere with their choices. They call you their god, because they are free to do as they please. The truth is you are nothing more than a lifeless idol."

Peak was trembling with rage as he made his final declaration. "I am a god! The people do my will!"

His protest came to an abrupt halt when the blackbird suddenly took flight and ejected a disgusting white liquid that landed on Peak's head.

Peak was deeply offended, yet after the

blackbird's visit, he had to face the truth. In spite of his new place of wealth, prominence, and the pretense of happiness, deep inside he was lonely, unfulfilled, and guilt ridden.

The seasons slowly changed from summer to autumn and the people prepared to celebrate the harvest and to give thanks to Peak for his many blessings. Peak looked forward to this celebration with great anticipation. He could only imagine what delicious and wonderful things the people would bring to show their love and devotion.

Finally, the time arrived and the celebration began. For days and nights, the singers and dancers paraded before his image. Peak, however, was not amused when the people began to perform unspeakable acts in his presence.

They burned strange-smelling incense, slaughtered animals, and mixed blood with wine. They drank from the cups and then poured the rest over the disgusted Peak. They made bonfires from the bushels of wheat and corn—grain that had been taken from the mouths of the poor—to dedicate to Peak.

Finally, the last night of the celebration arrived. Both men and women were completely intoxicated with the wine of perversion and sadistic merriment. The procession of priests walked slowly into the courtyard, singing as they came into the presence of the great Peak. The drums rolled like thunder and the horns and string instruments could be heard for miles around. A fire was lit in a large brass container that was laid the foot of the altar. The high priest raised his hands and a hush came over the crowd. The only sound that could be heard was the piercing cry of a newborn baby.

The baby screamed at the top of its lungs as the mother handed the child to the high priest who was dressed in a long, white robe stained with blood. The sinister-looking man raised the child as high as his arms would allow. He swayed back and forth while singing a mysterious song to an ominous melody. Horror engulfed Peak as he looked at the helpless baby and then at the leaping flames in the brass container. Peak trembled with fear.

"God, what have I done?" he whispered.

He was shaking uncontrollably as if an earthquake was emanating from the core of his being. Then, when he was not able to contain himself any longer, he cried out, "Noooooooo!" His mute screams filled the night air. "Nooooooo!"

Although his voice was beyond the range of humans, the cosmic echoes filled the atmosphere with a force that swept over the surrounding mountains and hillsides until they joined in one violent protest. Peak rocked back and forth as the baby came closer to the flames.

"Lord, God! Please forgive me! I am not a god. I am a fool. Please, have mercy, not for my sake but for the sake of the baby. Please, have mercy!" Peak cried out.

Suddenly, the ground in the courtyard began to shake. The high priest froze in his tracks. "This sacrifice is not acceptable!" he declared as the ground continued to shake. His heart was pounding as the shaking grew more violent.

The groans of people arrayed in elaborate garments soon turned to desperate screams as the wrath of God descended on the mountain courtyard. The rumbling grew louder and the ground began to split apart. The baby fell from the hands of the priest into his mother's arms.

Moments later, a rainstorm erupted, bringing thunder, lightning bolts, and hailstones that fell like a treasure chest of glistening diamonds. Peak did not resist or cry out as the avalanche of stones, dirt, and mud rolled down into the courtyard where he was standing.

Peak swayed like a garment caught in a strong gust of wind. With one final swaying motion, he toppled over the edge of the cliff and continued down the steep embankment, breaking into smaller and smaller pieces as he smashed against the jagged wall of stone.

Finally, what was left of Peak plunged headfirst into the raging river below. He sank into the muddy bottom, praying that he would never rise again.

CHAPTER 5

MUDDY
WATERS

Rivers of time passed quietly by ushering in
the new seasons with all of their splendors.
The winters came again and again, dressing
the countryside with lace garments of freshly
fallen snow. Soon, the springtime followed,
painting the hills and valleys on a canvas of
vivid colors.

Then a very special winter season
ended, breaking the stillness of the frozen

landscape. The melting snow poured down the mountainside, causing the riverbeds to overflow and teem with new life.

Hungry, speckled fish planted their eggs in the soft mud. In ritual fashion, families of beavers, birds, newborn cubs, and all other wildlife made their way down to the river's edge. They came to meet, greet, drink, and bathe, just as their ancestors had done before them.

"Is there no rest for the dead?" Peak groaned as the swarming activity of the river forced him to be pushed, tumbled, then rise and fall again and again without any apologies from the intruders for their rude behavior."

The blatant disrespect of commoners was so overwhelming that Peak did his best to will himself into a withdrawn state where the world around him no longer existed. "I will myself into nothingness. I am no longer alive. I am resting in my eternal grave. I will myself into nothingness. I will myself into nothingness," Peak chanted the words over and over, waiting for the intoxicating sensation of feeling invisible to overtake him.

One day in the midst of Peak's spoken ritual, he was rudely interrupted by a large clump of ebony mud that was shaking his head with disapproval. "If you're looking for a quiet grave of nothingness, you should never have landed yourself in this riverbed," he scolded Peak. "Rivers are the source of life, not death. So why don't you dig yourself out of that rut you're in and join the living?"

"Who are you?" Peak reeled at the intrusion.

"My name is Muddy Waters, but around here, they call me Mr. Mud for short."

"Well, Mr. Waters or Mud, or whatever your name is, falling into this muddy river certainly wasn't my idea. It was purely an accident."

Mr. Mud looked at Peak. "Sometimes, what you think is an accident is really one of life's divine appointments.

"You call this a life?" Peak fumed.

"Why of course it is. It may not be to your liking right now, but the funny thing about life is that it's always changing."

"What difference does it make if I'm alive when things are only changing for the worse?"

Mr. Mud was losing patience. "I only know what I know. And if you're still breathing, then it must be for a good reason."

"Name one." Peak frowned.

"If you start moving forward, sooner or later, I bet you'll run right into a bunch of reasons."

"I don't want to move forward," Peak insisted. "I just want to be left alone!"

A fresh smile appeared on Mr. Mud's face that resembled the finger painting of a small child. "Sounds like you need a big dose of hope."

"Hope?" Peak fumed.

"It's not that complicated," Mr. Mud said as he waved his thick, dark arms around, clouding up the water. "'Hope is believing for something that you can't see, 'cause if you can see it, then there's no need to hope' (Romans 8:24).

"Hope will give you a boost when you feel like you're running out of steam. So stop dwelling on past disappointments and have a little faith. Start believing that something good is gonna come your way, and it will!"

Peak wanted to escape from the annoying Mr. Mud, but the large, dark clump was blocking his way.

"That was a very nice speech, sermon, or whatever. Now if you'll excuse me, I'm going to go right out and conquer the world."

Mr. Mud laughed like someone beating on a loud bass drum. "I know you might feel trapped and think you don't have a future, but a lot of good things hit rock bottom. I ought to know, 'cause I am the bottom. Hahahaaaa!"

Peak let out a sigh as Mr. Mud's laughter rippled through the water.

"I see things fall in this river all the time," Mr. Mud continued. "It looks like they're so messed up that they'll never make it out of here. Then suddenly, the whole mess turns into a miracle and they rise right back up to the top."

In spite of the resistance in his heart, something began to stir inside of Peak. Now he was starting to really listen to what Mr. Mud was saying.

"God has a purpose and a plan for everyone, even a muddy bottom like me."

"What do you mean?" Peak's curiosity was growing.

"Don't you see? Without me, the rivers couldn't run their course. Just think what would happen to all the farms and villages without a river running through them with a big muddy bottom to guide the flow of water."

"But what purpose could God possibly have for a piece of broken stone?" Peak asked.

"Have a little faith, my friend! Life is full of surprises, so why don't you start moving on and see what tomorrow brings?"

"To tell you the truth, I'm too afraid to move on," Peak confessed.

"Afraid of what?" Mr. Mud's tone was gentle.

"Failing! Getting hurt again! Making stupid mistakes! That's what!"

Mr. Mud was smiling as if he had heard these words before. "Listen, my friend. In this life, we all fail at something, we all get hurt, and we all—including myself—make stupid mistakes. That's what life is all about. So get out there and start living again. You can do it!"

Mr. Mud gave Peak a loving push, forcing him out of his rut and onto the river's current that would carry him downstream to his destiny. He said a prayer as he watched him go. "May the God of hope fill you with all joy and peace as you trust in him, so that you may overflow with hope by the power of the Holy Spirit." Amen! (Romans 15:13).

"Be sure to look for the big oak tree! You can't miss her!" Mr. Mud shouted. "Her name is Morah. Tell her I sent you. And if you run into my no-count cousin Sludge, tell him I said to clean up his act! Hahaha."

Peak's journey downstream was not an easy one. It was slow and tedious and seemed to take forever. Under the scorching sun, the riverbed dwindled into a narrow stream, making it harder and harder for Peak to move. With all the starting and stopping, colliding with other stones and being entangled in roots, Peak was hot, exhausted, and discouraged. Not to mention there was no sign of an oak tree named Morah. He wanted to move forward, but each day brought less and less activity, and once again, he was discouraged and losing hope.

"I can't take this anymore! I'm stuck in this mud and I'm not going anywhere!" Peak cried out.

"God, I know we're not on the best of terms, but if I have been left here for a reason, then help me move forward so I can find it!"

There was no answer, and very slowly, Peak began to sink back into his muddy rut.

"Delaaays, delaaays, delaaays." The voice sounded like someone poking fun.

"Who's there?" Peak was startled.

"The name is Sludge!"

Peak could barely make out the dark-gray form lounging near the banks of the river. "Who are you and… what are you?" Peak asked.

"Like I said, my name is Sludge. You probably met my cousin Mud upriver. He didn't tell you about me?"

"Yes, I met Mr. Mud, and he did tell me about you. Now will you please tell me what you're talking about?"

"So now he's Mr. Mud." Sludge shook his head and laughed. "Well, like I was about to say: my job is to slow you down with some well-planned delays."

"But why? Why would you want to delay my travel?" Peak was confused.

"Oh, it's not me that's causing the delays. You see, delays are the servant's of God's perfect timing. I'm just here to make sure everything stays on track."

"On track? Is that supposed to be a joke?" Peak huffed.

"Listen, this is how it works," Sludge explained. "If you move too fast, then you'll arrive at your destination before your destiny is in place. If you move too slow, you'll miss your destiny because you're in the right place at the wrong time."

"So that's why everything around me dried up?" Peak asked.

Sludge shrugged his thick shoulders. "Look, I just work here. I know it's frustrating when something gets in the way of your plans. But you should really be thanking God for the delays."

"Thanking God? Why?"

Because delays hold everything in place until the timing is perfect."

"Perfect for what?" Peak yelled at Sludge.

"Perfect for God's purpose." He smiled at Peak.

"I have to go! It's past my naptime." Sludge looked up at the position of the sun in the sky, signifying he was checking on the time. "I'll be close by if you need me." He buried his head and disappeared.

As Peak lay stuck in the mud, he lost track of time. Suddenly, there was a gush of cool air. The soft wind pressed against the mud and trickles of water gently moved Peak into a shady spot near the edge of the riverbed.

Now Peak could hear singing that sounded like wind chimes in a breeze.

When he looked up, just above his head stood a tall, regal, oak tree smiling down at him from the banks of the river.

"You'll feel a lot better once my leaves fan away the heat," she said.

At first, he was speechless. Finally, the

words came out. "Are you Morah?" Peak stared up at the beautiful oak tree in disbelief.

"I am, indeed. Please forgive Sludge. He meant no harm. Sometimes, he can be overzealous about his work. Now that you are here, maybe I can keep you company while you are waiting to see what God has in store for you."

"I doubt if anything good is in store for me," Peak groaned. "I've been broken so many times that I can't imagine that everything that happened is part of a perfect plan."

Morah gave a faint laugh. "Dear one, if you did not have the faith to believe in a better future, you would have never made it this far down the river. You would have remained forever stuck in your discouragement. Now that you've made it this far, you must have enough faith to continue your journey until you fulfill your destiny." Morah hummed and swayed in the gentle breeze as if she was hiding some delightful secret.

"How can I have faith when there's hardly anything left of me? I was a great mountain peak, looking down on the entire world. Now

I'm nothing more than a worthless piece of stone," Peak moaned.

"But that's what faith is," Morah responded. "Something as small as a mustard seed believing that it can grow beyond the limits of possibilities. Miracles do happen, and with God, all things are possible (Mark 10:27)."

"Faith, miracles. It's all too much for me to understand." Peak wasn't sure if he was speaking out loud or talking to himself. But Morah answered anyway.

"A small stone like you has the potential for great miracles. You may never be a mountain peak again, but you might discover that God's will for you is something much greater."

Peak turned away, not wanting Morah to see the anger that was engulfing him. "I think I've heard enough for now," he mumbled.

Morah's final words were like a dose of unwanted medicine that Peak was forced to swallow.

"I understand," Morah said. "Just know that God can use you, just the way you are."

What she said did not sit well with Peak.

He closed his eyes and moved around until he managed to bury himself deeper into the mud.

The days passed slowly in the dwindling river. Each morning, Peak watched Sludge, who spent most of his time sitting on the side of the riverbank with his arms folded behind his head. Sometimes, he even whistled a tune. The annoying sight of Sludge sitting close by was a constant reminder to Peak that he was being held hostage in this dried-up riverbed.

For some strange reason, Morah became the one source of true peace in Peak's life. The way she stretched her branches to the heavens and sang along with the flocks of birds that rested on her limbs brought comfort to Peak's soul. They talked for hours at a time and then she would pray and recite God's word out loud, blessing all the inhabitants of the riverbed.

"Faith is the substance of the things we hope for, the evidence of things not seen... Without faith it is impossible to please God, for he who comes to God must believe that he exist and that he rewards those who seek him with their whole heart" (Hebrews 11:1–6).

Morah smiled down at Peak. "God is

faithful, and this river will flow again at His appointed time."

Even though Peak did not join in when the rocks cried out in praise, the words and melodies were slowly seeping into his heart. He often came close to rejoicing, but each time he tried, the memories of past failures always interrupted. "If only I could be free from this sorrow," Peak's words were full of heaviness.

Morah could clearly see the struggle that he was going through and she continued to encourage him. "I learned a long time ago that sorrow serves a very important purpose."

"What kind of purpose?" Peak wasn't sure he wanted to hear the answer.

"Sorrow is like a hole that life digs in you so that you will have a greater capacity for joy. The deeper the hole of sorrow, the greater the room you will have for joy."

Peak laughed bitterly. "Then I should be happier than anyone on earth!"

"Perhaps one day you will be." Morah stayed her course with great confidence. "I know you think I'm not making any sense, but with time, understanding will come."

"I don't think I'll ever understand the reasons for all the things that happened in my life," Peak argued.

Morah didn't reply. Instead, she looked toward heaven and prayed for Peak. "Help him to trust in your unfailing love, and let his heart rejoice in your salvation" (Psalm 13:5).

"Do you really think God is listening? Do you really think he cares about me?" Peak's words were filled with anger.

Morah stared at him. "Why are you holding on to bitterness and blaming God? Don't you know that you'll never be free to move on to the future if you keep holding on to the past?"

"How can I let go when the memories of what happened are with me day and night? How can I not be angry when God continues to punish me?" Peak fought back tears.

"Maybe what you see as God punishing you is really God perfecting you."

Morah paused as if the words on her lips were almost too difficult to speak. She stared into a distant place and time. "I too have gone through painful seasons that I thought would never end. I can still see the faces of the men that assaulted me. They came with sharp axes. Chopped my limbs and trunk until there was almost nothing left of me. Death waited for me to enter the grave, but my faith in God demanded that I fight to live. Through that terrible experience, I discovered that God's strength is made perfect in weakness" (2 Corinthians 12:9).

"My roots traveled deep into the earth searching for the scent of water. And when it seemed that all was lost, early one spring day, I found the living water I prayed for. Soon I began to grow again."

Once more Morah waved her branches in praise. "Now I am taller and stronger than I've ever been. What Satan means for evil, God can turn into our greatest blessing."

Peak listened intently without any resistance. Suddenly, a swift wind traveled down the side of the mountain. It blew hard against Morah until her leaves swirled in the air and filled the river below.

"The spirit of healing has come," Morah whispered in the wind. "The Lord is near the brokenhearted and saves those who have been crushed in spirit" (Psalm 34:18).

Peak felt anxious as he watched the heavens drape itself in a dark, satin robe. Then came a downpour of rain that was so intense that it quickly covered the dry, parched earth and filled the riverbed.

"She said the rain would come," Peak whispered to himself.

He watched intently as the storm kicked and screamed like an unruly child. With each flash of lightning, the horror of his great fall came exploding back to his memory.

The leaves in the water continued to swirl faster and faster as the pain and anguish overflowed from Peak's heart. *You'll never be free to move forward if you keep holding on to your past. It's up to you.* Morah's words echoed in his mind.

He could see the faces of the dreadful clouds that beat against him with snow and hail. "I hate you for what you did to me!" He shook his fist at the black clouds above. "I hate myself for being weak and letting you destroy me! God, where were you when I needed you? Why did you let this happen to me? Why?"

In spite of his angry words, the healing

wind of the Spirit continued to blow, penetrating his pain and guilt, soothing his grief.

Finally, the Spirit of the Lord revealed the answer to the question that had tormented him for so long. It was a painful moment as the truth that was buried deep in his soul rose to the surface of his mind. At last, he came face-to-face with the mystery of his fall.

It was pride. His pride made him believe that he was invincible and that he didn't need anyone—not even God.

Peak bowed down and made his confession. "Lord, now I realize that pride goes before destruction, and a haughty spirit before a fall (Proverbs 16:18). Please forgive my sins and cleanse me of all unrighteousness."

All through the night, the healing rain washed over him again and again.

Early the next morning, just as the dawn was breaking, Peak lay in the soft mud engulfed in a strange new feeling. "I'm not angry anymore. I'm free."

CHAPTER 6

A GLIMMER OF HOPE

By the time the healing work was completed, Peak and Morah had formed a lasting bond of friendship. She was his teacher and trusted secret keeper. With her encouraging words, Peak grew in his relationship with God.

"I'm beginning to know God's voice," Peak explained to Morah. "When He talks to me, it's like He's standing right next to me." Peak was overflowing with an unexplainable joy.

"He is present and He's been with you all along." Morah smiled. "His voice can be heard more clearly than ever when you spend time in His Word."

As always, Peak embraced Morah's wise counsel. "In my heart I want to do something big for God, but I feel so small and inadequate."

Morah looked down at Peak's small, rocky frame. "Love and kindness have nothing to do with size. Wisdom and knowledge cannot be measured by height or width. Powerful things can come in very small vessels."

"I still don't understand how God could possibly use me," Peak said as he sighed.

Once again, Morah offered a bit of homespun wisdom. "Start where you are, use what you have, and do what you can. God will do the rest."

Peak mouthed the words over and over. "Start where you are, use what you have, and do what you can. God will do the rest."

He took a long look at his surroundings, hoping to find the meaning in what Morah was saying. At first, his eyes could only see the dull, humdrum events that made up life in the river. But as time passed, the river began to take on an enchanting beauty that was hard for Peak to define. Clusters of crystals with geometrical patterns glistened in the water. Reed-like plants danced and swayed to the motion of the river's current. A green serpent with metallic, blue stripes slithered, by flashing a harmless gaze. Even a large, solitary turtle stopped to acknowledge Peak, mumbled a greeting, and then withdrew his head into his shell.

"I thought you were anxious to move on, embrace your destiny."

Peak recognized the familiar voice and turned to greet Sludge. "I think I'm learning to wait for God's perfect timing."

Sludge grinned. "When the time is right everything will flow. There will be no more delays."

Once again, Sludge slowly disappeared down the river's muddy banks.

With his days of splendor fading from his memory, Peak soon made friends among the other stones. There were the two flints: one big and one small. The residents often referred to them as Flint One and Flint Two. The Flint family was well known for their use as tools and weapons. They even possessed the power to start fires. But when Peak asked about their illustrious heritage, Flint One barely spoke a word. Flint Two only shrugged his shoulders.

There was also the flamboyant, fun-loving marble, with his dark-blue swirls and smooth, luxurious surface. "Let me tell you about the days I spent in the finest palace in all of the realm. It was invaded by rebels, but the marble pillars stood firm until reinforcements came to our rescue…"

Peak was so spellbound by the stories that it was hard to decide what was truth or fiction. Because of all of his adventures, the marble stone was given the name Captain Marble.

Morah confided in Peak that it was one reckless adventure too many that landed Captain Marble in the river.

The greatest evidence of Peak's transformation was the close relationship with a rival limestone called Limey. Long ago, Peak had developed a personal dislike for limestone because of his experience in the quarry. Until now, he had convinced himself that limestone were not to be trusted. Limey felt the same way about his granite rivals.

But things changed as they got to know each other.

"You don't remember me, do you?" Limey approached Peak as they worked together in the riverbed. Peak was puzzled.

"I was there in the courtyard when you sat as an idol. I was one of the large pillars that held up the temple." Limey tried to jar Peak's memory.

"Well, as you know, in those days I was a little self-absorbed, to say the least," Peak confessed.

"I thought I was pretty important myself." Limey smiled at the memory of his glory days. "Becoming a pillar in a great house was my life's dream. When the temple collapsed during the earthquake, I blamed myself for not being strong enough. Then I blamed you," Limey admitted."

"But when I saw how broken you were at the bottom of the river, I realized you didn't have enough power to cause a violent earthquake. Now I know it was God's doing."

From that time on, Peak and Limey were inseparable friends. They shared history and pain, but most of all, they shared healing.

Much to Peak's surprise, the stones were never without work to do. They were lively stones, laboring from sunup to sundown, improving the quality of life in the river. There were stones that gathered themselves together to filter out sand and other debris so the birds and animals could have clean water to drink.

When new plants sprouted along the edge of the banks, the stones held the tender branches in place until the stems and roots grew deep enough and strong enough to withstand the water's current.

The stones dug deep into the muddy bottom, creating a passage for the water to make its way to underground wells for storage during times of drought.

There were no more lonely hours, no more overwhelming feelings of emptiness. For this, Peak was grateful.

Things were quiet during the winter months. But in the early spring, there was a dramatic transformation. Peak could feel the tension as the other stones looked up at the snow melting on the mountainside.

"He'll be here soon," Flint One said to the others.

"Who will be here?" Peak asked.

"Chilly." Flint Two spoke the name but said nothing more.

"Who's Chilly?" Peak was a little uneasy.

"When you hear the loud sound of gushing water coming down from the mountains, then you will meet him for yourself," Flint One explained.

"He's not very nice," Flint Two added.

Peak looked up at Morah, who had her eyes fixed on the mountains. "You'll need to reinforce the younger trees and warn the animals to stay out of the river," she said to Peak.

"Okay," he responded, without fully understanding what was about to happen.

On the following morning, there was a sound like the distant roar of an approaching storm. As the sound grew louder, the silver fish began to nervously dart about. Frogs, turtles, and all other creatures made their way to the muddy banks.

Then it happened. The wild man known as Chilly lifted his arms high and raced toward the river below, roaring at the top of his lungs, "Coming throooough!"

Soon everything in the river was shoved, banged, and slammed about. As Chilly continued his merciless trek, he pushed everything in his path to the breaking point. Tree limbs, stones, fish, and plants were bruised, battered, and tossed in every direction.

"Hurry! Hold on to the roots of the trees!" Peak yelled to the frightened snails.

Captain Marble, Limey, Flint One, and Flint Two did their best to protect the young trees and plants growing along the river's edge.

"Gather more rocks to hold things in place!" Flint One yelled out to the others. But even the strong Flint brothers were no match for Chilly. The stones rolled and tumbled around like feathers in the wind. Peak closed his eyes and buried himself deep into the mud as the raging rapids continued its attack on the river.

The stronger plants, with flexible branches and deep roots, held on tightly as the raging waters tossed and bent them in every direction. The weaker plants, with shallow roots, were quickly broken and carried away by the strong current.

As the day drew to a close, Chilly finally came to rest. By the next morning, the spring sunlight warmed the icy waters. Needless to say, all the inhabitants of the river were in an uproar. They were deeply offended by Chilly's bullying. By the time Peak dug himself out of the mud, he found Limey with his fist raised, spewing out angry words at Chilly.

Captain Marble was even more upset as he addressed the intruder. "Do you have to make such a big splash every year when you come into the river? This kind of brutality is completely unnecessary."

Chilly sighed as if he was bored with the complaint. But Captain Marble wasn't done.

"You destroyed most of the plants and trees and the helpless fish have been carried away. What do you have to say for yourself?"

Chilly playfully slapped the water, sending ripples in every direction. "I see you're still here." He grinned at Captain Marble.

Limey gritted his teeth. "How can you make jokes? Don't you care about the damage you've done?"

Chilly had a smirk on his face. "Look, I'm just going with the flow!"

"Going with the flow? What's that suppose to mean?" Peak felt compelled to speak out.

Morah cleared her throat as if to interrupt the angry protestors. "What Chilly means by 'going with the flow' is that it's not his decision to come crashing into the river. He is only doing what God requires of him. You see, the current of water must be strong enough and fast enough to travel through the entire valley."

Chilly nodded with approval. "You're the closest to the mountain, so you get hit the hardest. I guess you'll just have to live with it!"

"If that's the case, then I'm moving

downstream!" Captain Marble was still furious.

"Maybe you should try it," Chilly answered sarcastically. "Then you can join the stones down river that are always complaining about how I don't bring them enough fresh water. Why is it so hard to find contentment in the place where you are?"

Chilly took one last look at the cluster of angry stones. "Look, everybody will face some hard knocks in life. But with all the knocking around, have you notice how smooth you're becoming?" Then he was gone.

Peak looked at his reflection in the water. In spite of the chaos, a noticeable change had taken place in what was left of him. All of his rough edges were gone and now he was a perfectly round, smooth stone.

Chapter 7

THE PAIN OF CHANGE

Joyful times returned to the river, but the difficult days always followed. The water, sand, and rocks continued to rub against Peak until his glistening surface was as smooth as glass.

As the years passed, Peak was finally coming to terms with the uncertainties of life. No longer was he anxious when there was too little water in the river or too much water. In times of difficulties, those who lived in the river began to see him as a rock of confidence.

It was a tradition in the river that those who needed guidance or encouragement always went to Morah. But more and more, she began to send those who were hurt, angry, and confused to talk with Peak.

"Why are you sending them to me?" Peak protested to Morah. "You're the wise one—not me!"

Morah smiled at Peak. "I think you've experienced enough of life's difficulties to help others find their way. Besides, these days, I need more time to talk to the Lord and to listen to what He is saying."

"But what about the river and those who need you?"

Morah almost chuckled. "God was taking care of this river long before I came along, and long after I'm gone, He will still be in charge.

Morah looked at Peak with deep affection. "Your life will be much longer than mine. Perhaps it's time for you to stop digging around in the mud and start helping those who are trying to find their way."

With a mysterious wave of her branches, the mantle was passed.

When Peak was not busy sharing his story and encouraging those who came to him for help, he and Limey worked side by side inspecting plants and stones and sorting out the debris that tumbled down from the nearby mountains during the spring rains.

"There's nothing new under the sun," Limey commented about the strange things that ended up in the river.

Flint One and Flint Two started an underwater garden. They collected vegetation of every kind. The Flints planted them and watched them grow, even though, from time to time, storms would rise with raging waters and destroy most of their tedious work. Nevertheless, Flint One and Flint Two had strong constitutions, so starting over again and again didn't seem to bother them in the least.

Captain Marble was more adventurous. He traveled downriver searching for mineral stones rich in copper, sulfur, and iron. Even azurite, gold, and silver nuggets were included in his collection. He was becoming an expert on stones of every kind and often helped those who were shy and insecure understand their true value.

"You mean I am really worth a great price?" A gold nugget covered with dull rock looked at Captain Marble in unbelief.

"Indeed you are!" Captain Marble proclaimed with great confidence. "You may not look like it on the outside, but on the inside, you shine with beauty. Men will wage wars to possess you."

"And what about me?" A turquoise stone anxiously approached Captain Marble, wanting desperately to be affirmed.

"You are stunningly beautiful, a precious gift to the world," he declared, turning the turquoise stone around to get a better look.

When the swift waters came, as they always did, Captain Marble would release his precious mineral stones to travel down the swift currents of life.

"Make me proud!" he shouted, saluting them as they swirled away.

It was a strange and ferocious summer storm that broke Peak's quiet existence in the river. He, Limey, and Captain Marble could tell by watching the sky that a dark and ominous event was about to unfold. Flint One and Flint Two bowed their heads and whispered a prayer. Peak's heart was troubled, but he could not understand the reason for such strong feelings. He had survived many storms, yet there was something about what was looming overhead that made him pray for God's mercy.

"Answer me when I call to you, my righteous God. Give me relief from my distress; have mercy on me and hear my prayer" (Psalm 4:1).

Finally, the rain came down harder than the howling tears of a fallen angel. Thunder rolled across the turbulent sky like an army of warriors. The river swelled to capacity and then overflowed into the forest, the fields, the farms, and the villages.

The turbulent waters washed away everything that was weak, broken, and useless. The same raging waters carried rich deposits of topsoil, minerals, and other nutrients that enriched the land.

The earth moaned like a woman in labor, while thunder and lightning lashed out over the hillsides. Peak helplessly watched as the wind and rain danced together in a stormy gale.

Even Morah, who was known for her nerves of steel, was visibly shaken by the raging storm. The stones gathered beneath her deep roots as the waters rose higher and higher.

Suddenly, Peak's fear fled in the face of an overwhelming sense of courage. "We have to build a dam. It's the only way to save the farms and villages at the foot of the mountain."

"That's insane!" Limey protested. "There's nothing we can do. This is a hurricane."

"We have to try!" Peak began to hatch his plan.

While the other stones were still debating, Flint One and Flint Two moved toward the middle of the river and harnessed rocks, pieces of trees, and even dead animals that drowned in the flood of water. Peak, Limey, and Captain Marble quickly joined them. But the harder they worked, the higher the waters rose.

The clouds raised their thunderous voices in laugher and then came lower to the river and glared at Peak. "You're wasting your time," they mocked. "You are powerless against our strength. If you build a dam, we will wash it away. If you try to escape, we will overtake you!"

Peak stared back at his enemies. "I wasn't afraid of you then and I'm not afraid of you now! If tens of thousands come against me I will not fear, the Lord will arise and deliver me" (Psalm 3:6).

The clouds were disarmed by the boldness of Peak's words. They grumbled and then rolled away.

"To God be the glory!" Limey shouted as he stacked more branches and rocks onto the makeshift dam.

In the midst of the excitement, there was a very loud noise. It was like God himself roared from the heavens until every living thing stood still in his presence.

In the moment that followed, Peak discovered the source of the earth-shattering sound. Morah had been struck squarely in the heart by a bolt of lightning. Her limbs jerked violently while the weight of the heavy rain forced her trunk to split completely in half. The rain-soaked earth easily released her deep roots, and the regal oak tree fluttered about like a wounded dove.

For a moment, Morah straightened herself, as if she were determined to maintain her dignity to the very end. Like two gracious handmaidens, the wind gently embraced Morah's broken body and slowly laid her down into the swollen river.

Peak watched in silent agony as Morah surrendered to the swirling tide.

"No!" Flint One cried out. "No!" He pounded hard against his chest.

The heavy rain continued to fall as the five stones made their way to where Morah had fallen. One by one, they gathered around her. As Peak came closer, he could see that Morah was still clinging to life. He moved close to her, praying that he would find the right words. "Are you in pain?" he asked.

"No. I can't feel anything at all. She was trembling as she reached out and touched him.

A strange sense of peace came over Peak as he settled in beneath her broken branches. "I'll be right here beside you, just as long as you need me," he whispered. He looked up at the dark clouds that were hiding their faces in shame.

The next day, the rain stopped and the waters began to recede. Morah was still barely alive when the sun broke through the clouds.

"That's what I was waiting for." She smiled at Peak and the others. "To see the sun one last time. How dare the storm think it could outlast me?"

Peak smiled through his tears. It was good to know that his dear friend was still feisty. Captain Marble washed the mud from Morah's face and straightened what was left of her limbs. Flint One and Flint Two stood at attention like an honor guard watching over their fallen leader. Limey buried himself in the mud, not wanting to face this final moment.

Suddenly, Morah looked straight up at the sky. Her eyes were filled with surprise and wonder.

"Look! Do you see it?"

Peak and the others looked up and saw nothing but the clear, blue sky.

Morah spoke just above a whisper. "There's a river in the sky, a river of life. It's as clear as crystal flowing from the throne of God and of the Lamb... On each side of the river there's a tree... a tree of life, full of fruit, and the leaves have the power to heal the nations" (Revelation 22:1–3).

Morah was radiant as she she continued to gaze at the sky. Then she took one last deep breath. "I can hardly believe my eyes!" She gasped with excitement. "It's Jesus, and he's calling for me, to plant me near His throne.

"How marvelous!" she whispered, and then her spirit quietly departed.

In the days that followed, the inhabitants of the river mourned Morah's passing with sorrowful tears. Then early one morning, two men from the nearby village walked by the river, each of them carrying an ax.

"So here lies our blessing from heaven," one of the men said, looking at Morah.

"If it had not been for this fallen tree blocking the river, we would have lost everything."

The man ran his hand over her broken trunk. "This is beautiful oak. It will be perfect for replacing the roof of the church that was destroyed by the storm."

"Indeed," his friend said as he nodded his head. "This fallen tree is perfect for God's purpose."

CHAPTER 8

FAITH
LEAPERS

When Morah's made her journey to a distant heaven, life in the river seemed to have lost its meaning.

Peak drifted about, pretending to be busy but mostly doing nothing. Captain Marble talked of moving on in search of new adventures. But it wasn't hard to see that his taste for adventure had dulled.

Limey spent most of his time reflecting

on the past. "Remember the days when the temperatures soared and we gathered beneath Morah's branches as she fanned away the heat?"

Flint One and Flint Two shook their heads in agreement.

Peak glared at Limey and the others. "What good does it do to talk about the past when it only brings back bad memories?"

"They weren't all bad!" Limey insisted. "Like the time the snow covered Morah and she looked like she was wearing a long white robe—"

"Stop your chatter and find something useful to do!" Peak lashed out.

"You can't tell me what to do!" Limey grumbled.

"That's enough!" Flint One banged his fist against a rock. "This is not how Morah would have wanted us to treat each other."

Peak looked at Flint One. "You're right. I'm sorry, Limey. If talking about her makes you feel better, then I have no right to stop you."

Limey looked at Peak. "I'm sorry too. I

should have realized that talking about her might bother you."

"Group hug." Captain Marble joked with the circle of friends. Suddenly, he had a gleam in his eye. "You know what I think? I think we're all in a rut. Why not take a trip down the river?"

"I could certainly use a vacation, but I'm not sure I can spare the time," Limey explained.

"And what if a storm comes and we're not here to protect everyone?" said Flint One.

"And who's going to watch over my underwater garden?" Flint Two asked.

"Listen to yourselves," Captain Marble interrupted. "You're stuck in the mud and I'm stuck with you."

Peak found strength in Captain Marble's words. "We need to break free and see what God has for us beyond this little spot in the river. Who knows? We might not want to come back to this miserable place."

"And who says we have to stay in this river? There's a great big world out there." Captain Marble's mind was racing.

"So what's it going to be?" Peak was fired up!

"We should leave at the break of dawn," Flint One insisted.

So it was that in the light of the new day, the five stones made their way to the deep center of the river, where a strong current carried them to an uncertain destiny.

At first, it was smooth sailing. Peak was enjoying the turns and tumbles that propelled him downstream. "This is awesome!" Limey shouted to Captain Marble as the rapids grew stronger and the ride picked up speed.

Flint One and Flint Two grunted with excitement as they were tossed into the air and then plunged into the river's deep bottom.

Things were going quite well until an unexpected event met them head on. As they traveled around a sharp bend, there it was: a raging waterfall that would carry them over a steep cliff and into the turbulent waters below.

"If we hurry, we can escape to the rocks near the riverbank!" Limey yelled.

Peak didn't answer. He had already made

up his mind that wherever the river carried him, he would accept it as God's will.

"Don't be afraid!" Peak yelled to the others. "Just let go! Whatever happens, we're in God's hands."

No sooner than the words were spoken, the five stones exploded over the edge of the cliff as if they were being shot from a cannon.

Peak's mind flashed back to the icy storm that had broken him in two and landed him in the valley below. Then to the courtyard where he stood as an idol and the earthquake that shattered him into broken pieces and plunged him into the river. In spite of his life flashing in front of him, he had no fear of dying.

Like a newborn baby being forced from its mother's womb, a burst of water pushed him forward, then forward again and again until he swirled into a dark state of unconsciousness.

When he awoke, Peak was alone in a shallow, slow-moving part of the river.

"Limey, Marble, Flint One and Two, where are you?" Peak's voice echoed throughout the valley that surrounded the pool of water.

For hours on end, he moved about in the

shallow waters in search of his friends, but there was no sign of them anywhere.

A chill ran through him as he thought about the possibility of never seeing his friends again. Now he realized that allowing God to direct his path was more than he bargained for.

Even worse, what if the trek down the raging river had separated Flint One and Flint Two forever? What about poor Limey and Captain Marble? Fear began to wrestle with his faith and soon his heart was in a fierce tug of war.

He prayed quietly within himself. *I will trust you Lord and lean not to my own understanding! In all my ways, I will acknowledge you that you may direct my path (Proverbs 3:5).*

"Where was God when you fell from the mountaintop?" voices of doubt and fear challenged him.

"All things are working together for the good—" (Romans 8:28). Peak was about to complete his sentence when he caught a glimpse of a human shadow standing next to the water's edge.

Peak's heart was pounding like a drum as a boy, who was almost the size of a man, stepped into the water.

"God has not given me a spirit of fear, but of power and love and a sound mind" (2 Timothy 1:7). Peak had never spoken these words out loud before, but now all that he learned at the feet of Morah was taking on a new meaning.

As he struggled to find more words of faith to keep his fear at bay, the boy reached down and plucked Peak from the water. He held him in the palm of his hand, wiping away the water and mud, then studied his strong surface.

Peak prayed that the boy would toss him back into the water, but instead, the boy did the unthinkable. He opened a small, leather pouch that was tied to his belt and dropped Peak into the darkness.

Peak would have been completely engulfed by the terror, but the boy began to sing a song that renewed his faith. He knew at that moment that even in this strange place, God was with him.

The young boy continued to wade through

the shallow river, humming and singing and plucking stones from the water and then tossing most of them back. Once again, the pouch opened and, to Peak's surprise, Captain Marble made his way down the leather slide and landed next to his old friend.

"Only God! Only God!" Captain Marble shouted for joy.

"Have you seen any of the others?" Peak asked.

"No. You're the first. What is this place?" Captain Marble asked.

"God only knows," Peak answered as the darkness of the pouch covered them.

Flint Two was the next one to find his way into the dark pouch. "I can't find my brother! I've got to find my brother!" He tore at the walls of the leather pouch, trying to break free.

"Don't worry; we'll find him!" Peak tried to reassure Flint Two. "We found each other, and together, we will find your brother."

As the hours passed, Flint Two grew quiet. Peak was convinced that the boy's singing had a calming effect on all of them.

The singing and the dark closeness of the pouch soon lulled them all into a restless sleep. When the boy stopped singing, the bright light of day filled the pouch. Peak and the others prayed that, once again, they would be reunited with their friends.

Their prayers were answered when Limey came tumbling into the pouch. Fearful and out of breath, he could hardly believe that he had found his friends. "Where did all of you come from, and how did you get here?"

"Your guess is as good as ours," Captain Marble answered.

As the pouch was closing, Flint Two desperately tried to scramble to the top. "No wait! Don't close it! I have to get out and look for my brother!" he shouted.

As the darkness closed in, Flint Two was furious. "This is all your fault!" he yelled at Peak. "You and your big ideas. If we had stayed where we were, I would have never lost my brother!"

"You can't blame this on Peak! No one forced you to come with us," Limey argued.

"Calm down, Flint Two," Captain Marble

added. "Apparently, this boy has some sort of plan. And for whatever reason, he selected us. Pretty soon, he'll find Flint One and we'll all be together again."

"Then what?" Flint Two was still anxious. "I mean, why us? Where is he going, and what is he going to do with us?"

Peak groaned in frustration. "Why are you so afraid? We've already been broken, blasted, crushed, and buried in the mud and dirt. We have nothing left to fear. If the boy picked us, it must be for a good reason."

Flint Two answered quickly. "I fear life without my brother, and I fear the unknown!"

What Limey was about to say came as a surprise to everyone because he had never uttered the words before. "I think we should pray."

"Limey, you want to pray?" Captain Marble joked.

"This is no time for folly." Peak stopped Captain Marble. "Limey is right. We need to ask God to help us and to show us what to do."

"And we need God to help me find my brother," Flint Two added.

"You'd better lead us," Captain Marble said to Peak.

"Lord, you are our rock, our fortress, and our deliverer. In you we take refuge. You are our shield and the horn of our salvation. You are our stronghold. Lord, in you, we put our trust" (Psalm 18:2).

When the prayer ended, there was a long silence. Peak listened intently and the boy continued to sing. Suddenly, the boy's mood changed and instead of singing he shouted. "The Lord is my light and my salvation, so why should I be afraid?" (Psalm 27:1).

"Who is he talking to?" Limey asked.

"I think he's talking to someone or something that's about to come against him. He's letting his enemies know that he's not afraid," Peak answered.

CHAPTER 9

FIVE SMOOTH STONES

Even though the pouch that the boy was carrying was closed, there was still enough of an opening at the top to see faint streams of light. Peak also noticed that the smell in the air was changing. Earlier in the day, the air was crisp and clean, but now there was a faint smell of fire and smoke.

The boy was no longer singing, and a distant rumbling grew louder and closer.

"Is that the sound of a storm?" Limey asked the others.

"Maybe it's a earthquake." Captain Marble was bewildered.

Instead of being afraid, Peak could feel a sense of excitement stirring inside of him. "It sounds like an army to me."

"You mean, like soldiers and fighting?" Flint Two asked.

"I'm not really sure." Peak continued to listen.

When a sudden blast shook the boy and the roar of angry voices could be clearly heard, there was little doubt that they were close to a battleground.

The boy began to move faster. As his feet splashed through the water, he shouted back at the voices, "I am not afraid! Though your army surrounds me, I am not afraid!" (Psalm 27:4). The boy chanted the words over and over.

There was so much power in his words that, in the darkness of the pouch, the stones began to chant with him. "I am not afraid! I am not afraid!"

Suddenly, the boy stopped in his tracks and once again reached into the stream. When the pouch finally opened, they could see Flint One glistening in the light.

"Put me down!" Flint yelled at the boy as he tossed him into the leather bag with a loud thump.

"Brother, you're safe!" Flint Two shouted with joy.

"Is everyone here?" Flint One asked.

"We're all here!" Peak assured him.

"This is not a good place to be," Flint One explained. "When I was in the shallow waters, I could see smoke, fire, and an army of men marching into battle. We've got to find a way to escape," he urged the others.

Peak was quick to respond. "If you could all get together and push me to the top of the pouch, maybe I can figure out where we are and we can come up with a plan."

"Good idea," Limey said, climbing on top of the others.

"I'm the strongest, so I'll stay on the bottom," Flint One added. As he strained to lift the other stones, he whispered a prayer.

"Lord, stand under us. For if you stand under us and lift us high, we will have understanding and know what to do."

Peak climbed upward until he finally reached the opening of the pouch. What he saw took his breath away. Standing in the middle of a war-torn field loomed a creature that was larger than any man he had ever seen. He was shouting threatening words.

"I am Goliath, champion of the Philistines," the giant of a man boasted. When his eyes fell on the frail young boy, he cursed and roared like a lion. "Am I a dog that you come to me with sticks?" (1 Samuel 17:43)

"What sticks?" Peak looked out at the boy.

Once again, his heart was in his mouth as he saw what was in the boy's hand. "He has a slingshot!" Peak yelled to the others. "He's going to fight a giant with a slingshot."

"A giant?" The others were in shock.

"We've never seen a giant. What does he look like?" they shouted back at Peak.

"He's as tall as one man standing on top of another. His face looks more like a beast than a human."

Flint Two used his strength to dig small holes in the side of the pouch. He and the others looked out and discovered that what Peak was telling them was even worse than what he had described.

"It's a giant all right, and he's coming toward the boy." Flint Two warned.

"What are we going to do?" Limey tried not to panic.

Before anyone could answer, the boy shouted back at the giant. "I am David, the son of Jesse, defender of Israel. You come to me with a sword and a spear, but I come to you in the name of the LORD of host! I will strike you and take your head from you!" (1 Samuel 17:45).

"Strike him with what? All you have is a slingshot!" Peak found himself talking to the boy.

Suddenly, the reality of the boy's plan hit Peak like a lightning bolt. *"You're going to use a stone and slingshot to try to kill a giant?"*

When the others realized what was about to happen, they panicked and fell apart. Peak came tumbling back into the pouch.

"We've got to find a way to stop him, or that giant will kill him for sure!" Peak said to the others.

"Didn't you hear what the boy said?" Flint One interrupted. "He said the Lord was going to deliver him. This matter is in God's hands, not ours. Now I know why he plucked us from the river. If he's planning on using a slingshot, then he needs stones."

With those words, everyone grew quiet.

"A slingshot and a stone? Dear God, I know that with you the mission is possible?" Peak whispered a prayer. "Lord, help me to understand and accept your plan."

Suddenly, the small pouch was filled with a holy visitation. It was the Spirit of the Lord instantly transforming them into fearless warriors, invincible and full of faith.

Above the thunderous sound of marching soldiers, they could hear the Lord speaking. "The difficulties of life have rubbed against you and you have rubbed against each other. Now you are perfect stones.

"Peak will become my instrument to defeat the giant, but all of you will play a part in the victory. Peak will be unwavering in the midst of the battle because Limey has taught him faithfulness and loyalty. He will face the unknown with no fear of the outcome, because Captain Marble has passed on to him the spirit of adventure. Finally, he will be fearless and courageous because he carries with him the strength of Flint One and Flint Two.

"I have called each of you for a time such as this," said the Lord. Then there was silence and the five smooth stones knew it was time to complete their divine calling.

"Lord, use us for your glory," Peak whispered.

"We are all ready," the others agreed.

In the next moment, the pouch opened wide and dust and smoke covered the stones as the boy's words rang out. "Now all the earth will know that there is a God in Israel!" (1 Samuel 17:47).

Flint One and Flint Two lifted Peak onto their shoulders until he was close to the boy's fingers.

"We will be with you," Limey cried out.

"All for one and one for all!" Captain

Marble cheered him on. When the boy touched Peak, there was no doubt that he was the one. Peak felt as bold as a lion as the young warrior placed him in the fold of the slingshot and began to twirl him in the air.

David gave a loud shout as he fearlessly ran toward Goliath. "All those gathered here will know that it is not by sword or spear or javelin that the Lord saves; *for the battle is the Lord's,* and he will give all of you into our hands" (1 Samuel 17:47).

Peak could feel his soul take flight as David hurled him into the air. For the last and final time, he saw the vision of himself falling from the top of the mountain peak. But this time, he was rejoicing, thanking God that He did not leave him in a place where he was of no use to anyone—not even himself. He thanked God for allowing him to discover his true purpose.

As he soared through the air, he could feel God filling him with more power than he had ever imagined. "The battle is the Lord's! He will give you into my hands!" Peak cried out as he hit the giant in his forehead like a torpedo.

There was a loud crashing sound as he smashed through bone, muscle, and flesh until he passed through the back of the giant's head and fell to the ground below.

Time seemed to stand still. Then Peak heard a voice speaking from heaven. "Well done, my good and faithful servant. Enter into your rest. You have fulfilled your purpose."

-End-

"For I know the plans I have for you,"
declares the LORD, "plans to prosper
you and not to harm you, plans to
give you hope and a future."
—Jeremiah 29:11

ADDITIONAL BOOKS BY
TERRI MCFADDIN-SOLOMON

Only A Woman – Tapping into God's Power
Random House Publishing

Sapphire and Other Precious Jewels: Discovering your jewel type and what makes you shine.
Random House Publishing

Read Terri's uplifting messages at:
www.Hopestreetblog.org

Join Terri's Fan Page on Facebook:
Terri McFaddin-Solomon

For speaking engagements and book signings:
TMcFaddinsolomon@gmail.com
Office: 310.327.4151